HER ROCKSTAR BILLIONAIRE

BAD BOY BILLIONAIRES - BOOK 2

JESSA JAMES

GET A FREE BOOK!

Join my mailing list to be the first to know of new releases, free books, special prices and other author giveaways.

http://freehotcontemporary.com

Her Rockstar Billionaire: Copyright © 2017 by Jessa James as Rock Me

All Rights Reserved. No part of this book may be reproduced or transmitted in any form or by any means, electrical, digital or mechanical including but not limited to photocopying, recording, scanning or by any type of data storage and retrieval system without express, written permission from the author.

Published by Jessa James
James, Jessa
Her Rockstar Billionaire

Cover design copyright 2017 by Jessa James, Author
Images/Photo Credit: Deposit Photos: VitalikRadko; 4045qd; Ssilver

This book was previously published as Rock Me

1

Every guy's got a girl that got away. One that rocked his world then fucked up his life. Yeah, I had one. Crystal Kerry. Shit. Just thinking her name was like driving a stake into my heart. Made my balls ache. She'd been perfect. My fucking high school sweetheart. Yeah, sweetheart.

I'd forgotten how fucking crowded New York was and had to cut through all the people on the sidewalk. Shit, it was insane. But, I was a face in a crowd. I wasn't Kit Buchanan, lead singer for Nightbird. I was just a guy lost in a sea of humanity. Thank fuck.

My thoughts were on Crystal and I didn't need a fan to grab hold and want a selfie or an autograph across her tits. I wanted to wallow in the one that got away. No, the one I pushed away and crushed, like a tank rolling over a soft, sweet, innocent kitten.

Crystal had been the one. Had been kind and gentle, always a smile for me since the first day of tenth grade. She'd transferred to Whitfield Prep as a scholarship student. Our classmates knew she was from the wrong side of the tracks. Poor. They'd sniffed out her blue-collar background, even though she looked like everyone else in the navy and green school uniform.

It had been hard for her, being new. Being beautiful. All the girls who'd been flirting—and fucking all the guys, suddenly had competition. Not that Crystal ever did anything. Just being pretty was enough. The guys, they called Crystal fresh meat. With her blond hair and pale blue eyes, she was as upper crust looking as everyone else. But unlike her classmates, she didn't know her effect on others. Had no idea she was hot. Not just average hot, that any teenage boy would want to bang, but night after night of wet dreams hot. Or jerking off in the shower just thinking about her perky tits and long legs hot.

That was fine for me to lust after, but not anyone

else. Especially not the assholes on the lacrosse team who'd made it their mission to see who'd fuck her first. They'd wanted that scholarship cherry and put bets on it.

I'd shut that shit down fast. My fists landed me with a three-day suspension, but I would have done it again in a heartbeat. No one was going to touch Crystal. No one...but me. She was mine. I knew it the first fucking time I saw her.

My parents had given me hell for getting into the fight. Hell for the suspension. Hell for the hours I spent playing guitar and writing music. I guess I dished it right back. For not being the prodigal son, the future CEO of Bullshit Buchanan Manufacturing, for not being a typical Buchanan. Hell, I'd been born with a silver spoon, but I'd spit it out and grabbed hold of a guitar instead. I'd been the fucking black sheep of the family. Still was. And living in that house after my two older brothers graduated from Whitfield and went on to Ivy League schools, the pressure had been on to measure up.

Whatever. I'd given up the chances for that when I was ten and wanted to take guitar lessons instead of playing Beethoven on the piano. I knew I'd never measure up. It hadn't been worth the effort.

As for Crystal, she'd wanted to succeed at Whitfield. Hell, it had been her chance, her opportunity to get out of the shit hole household she had. With a mother who was a doormat to a father who drank too much and held too few jobs, she'd known it was her escape. And she fucking took it. Got A's in all her classes, was valedictorian. She managed to do all this even with me following her around like a lovesick fool. But I loved her, protected her. She was my life and I was so much more than just her boyfriend. I was her best friend. She'd told me everything. Given me everything.

Yeah, she'd taken one look at me and melted. Somehow, by some fucking miracle, she'd fallen in love with my rough edges, the fact that I didn't fit in, didn't give a fuck. She knew I was her protector, that I'd do anything for her. We might've been each other's firsts, but I hadn't taken that scholarship cherry. No. She'd given it to me one night in the back of my pickup. We'd been in love. Even said the words. I'd spilled my guts as she sank down on my lap, naked and wet and too much for my seventeen-year-old body to resist. Crystal and Kit. We were inseparable. I knew I didn't deserve her. I was a spoiled silver spoon. I had never worked as hard as she had to. She'd been smart, so fucking smart, and I did what I could to keep her safe from the jealous bitches, and away from the jocks that noticed the same things I did. She wasn't just smart, she's was gorgeous, all curves and a killer smile.

I was the worst of them all. One quick smile, one hot kiss, and I would do anything she said, including study. And so perhaps she'd fucked me into graduating. Got my grades up so I could get my diploma, and listen to her sweet valedictorian speech. She'd dragged me along in her wake until we were both on our life paths, until she met me one Friday night with the news she'd gotten the scholarship to Stanford, that she was going to give it up for me.

It was then, I knew. I was no good for her. I was a dead end. I wasn't going to college. Hell, my parents had been threatening to cut me off if I went ahead with my plan to make a career in music. And I didn't mean the fucking symphony.

No, Crystal was going places. But not with me. So, I'd cut her loose the only way I knew how. I made sure news spread that I'd fucked Lindsay Mack, that while I took Crystal's virginity, I hadn't given her my heart.

I didn't touch Lindsay. But Crystal didn't know that.

My cell rang, bringing me back from the past. I pulled it from my pocket as I weaved around a woman pushing a stroller.

"What?" I barked into the phone.

"The sound check's set for four." Tia Monroe was a good band manager, but she could be a pain in the ass.

"Fine. I'll be there. Might be a few minutes late." I had no idea how long I would need if I was going to see Crystal again.

"Late? Why?"

"I have something to do." *Someone to see.*

I heard Tia say something else, but I tuned her out. Ended the call. Thought of Crystal. Tia and the band could wait. I'd devoted the past ten years of my life to tour buses and recording studios, they could wait thirty fucking minutes so I could get a glimpse of Crystal again. Knowing we were in the same town brought it all back.

Shit, after ten years it gutted me to remember the look on her face when I'd said what I'd done. What I'd *supposedly* done. Lindsay Mack had slept her way through our entire class and didn't care if I spread lies. Hell, she'd hated Crystal and was more than happy to strike her down the only way she could.

With tears streaming down her pale cheeks,

she'd turned and run away. Ran right out of my life for good. On to Stanford. Graduate school. And then some. She'd hated me, probably still did, but I could deal. She was too damn good for me, always had been. She could hate me and live her dreams.

She'd done just what she'd set out to do. Succeed. Hell, she'd done that. That was why I stopped in front of the three-story chain book store on Fifth Avenue. She was here for a book signing. I'd lost track of her when she left for California, but just six months ago, I'd turned on the television to see her sitting next to the most famous late night talk show host in the city. The novel she'd written a couple of years ago, had hit the *New York Times* list, big time. Her story sold in a multi-million-dollar deal and the hottest asshole in Hollywood was sitting next to her, playing the spy-thriller hero she'd dreamed up in her head. Fucker touched her shoulder, flirted with her. And she smiled back, but it was a smile I knew. Brittle. Stressed. So beautiful my cock rose to attention as I watched her, those blue eyes, those pink lips. She blinked, and laughed, made all the right motions for the audience, but I knew Crystal. My girl didn't like to be the center of attention.

And she was still mine. I knew every inch of her body, how she liked to be touched, kissed, fucked.

She was famous. Rich. She was no longer from the wrong side of the tracks. Hell, she made her own fucking tracks.

I was so damn proud of her. What were the chances I'd be in town on tour the same time she was here? When I'd seen her face on a huge-ass billboard, I knew I had to go. I had to see her, to see an expression on her face other than the heartbreak I'd caused her. Those sad eyes, the tears, had haunted me for a decade. I couldn't let her give up Stanford for me, but that didn't mean watching her walk away hadn't ripped my fucking heart out.

The store was huge. Three floors. It was packed with fans wanting a book signed by Crystal. To hear her give a talk about her characters, how she came up with the incredible plot. These people might have read her work, loved it, but I was her biggest fan. Hers. Not her story. Hell, they hadn't walked away from her to save her.

The ground floor was too crowded to get anywhere near her. Hell, I barely made it through the revolving door. The line was long and it snaked and curved. Spotting a stairwell that went to the second floor, I aimed for the balcony where I could look down and get a glimpse of her. I knew from the press photos she still wore her glasses. Still had the blond hair, the gorgeous blue eyes. She'd gotten older, grown from a girl to a woman. Wore make up. Heels, fancy clothes. No prep school uniform or cherry lip gloss.

Settling in, I leaned against the railing to look down. There she was. Fuck, my heart skipped a beat just seeing her again. The first time in ten years. The pictures didn't do her justice. While they showed only the confident woman that wrote that killer book, it hid her personality. The introvert who smiled because she had to. The quiet personality that liked a night in with a movie much better than one surrounded by hundreds of rabid fans.

I saw the tenseness in her shoulders even as she smiled and chatted with fans, signing her autograph over and over again. The sleek hair, the pretty blue dress, the fancy heels. It was all frosting. God, I wanted to strip her bare, to reveal the real Crystal. To find her again, to make her mine once more.

And when she turned to talk with a woman who stood behind the table next to her, perky and bubbly with her red hair and equally red dress, she somehow glanced up. Saw me. *As if she knew I was here.*

Her eyes widened. Her smile slipped. The pen slipped from her fingers. Those blue fucking eyes held mine and I knew. Like a fucking sucker punch to the gut, she was going to be mine again. I'd walked away once. Ten years ago, I'd had nothing to offer her. I'd let her go.

I couldn't do it again.

2

*rystal*

I HAD no idea so many people would show up. Vi had said it was going to be big, but this? This was almost a mob. And all to see me? God, I wasn't sure if I could smile anymore. No, I wasn't being a bitch about my success. My book had done so much better than I ever imagined. I never expected to get an agent, an agent who sold it to a New York publisher. Hell, an agent who sold the movie rights to one of the top producers in Hollywood. I'd never expected to be sitting on the late show circuit next to one of the hottest actors in the world. The movie was set to be a blockbuster. A stunning, too beautiful to be real, Academy Award winning actress was playing the female lead. My book!

Yeah, I'd wanted to be a writer, but this? This was crazy. I wanted to just get back to my hotel room and take a shower, put on my yoga pants and t-shirt and chill with a good book and a glass of wine. No noise. No smiling. Hell, no contact with anyone. I needed some peace and quiet. The energy of the crowds was overwhelming. The attention literally made me sick to my stomach. And that was one thing that had never changed. Yes, I'd grown up, learned how to deal with public appearances, but that only meant I needed a bubble bath and bottle of wine to save my sanity afterward.

As part of a three-month press tour, all I could do was smile and sign. Make small talk. Smile for selfies. Hug. Touch. Shake hands. My publicist, Vivian, had it all worked out. Thank god. I wouldn't want her job, but she loved taking care of all the crazy details. Of me. Sure, she was on payroll, but she was also my friend. Except for right now, when she handed me another book to sign.

"Almost done," she whispered. I was about to nod and turn back to the next person in the line when I saw him.

Him.

Holy fuck. Kit Buchanan.

I swear my heart leapt out of my chest. He was looking at me. No, staring so intently I swear I felt it to my core. Kit was here... for me. He wasn't in line, just watching.

Then he gave a slight nod. Nothing more. His dark hair slipped over his forehead. It was longer than when we were in high school, but I'd seen him since then on cover after cover of the gossip magazines. While I'd hit it big with my book, Kit had turned his rock star dreams into reality. From what I'd read in magazines, he'd worked his ass off with his band mates, playing small gigs for years. Then they'd written a song, *Angel,* the type of song that brought around the major record labels. They signed. Hit the big time. Platinum albums, awards, concerts around the world.

Women. Women in every city, a different one on his arm every night. Wild parties, fucking. It was all described in article after article about the famous Kit Buchanan. I read every word, gobbled it all up, even using a Google search notification to feed the images to me like a junkie. Evidently, I was a masochist. Every image hurt. Every smile, every groupie hanging on his arm. He'd been linked to models and Broadway starlets, fashion designers and other musicians. Every one of them looked up at him the way I used to. He was a god, a fucking sex god. And now, the famous lead singer of Nightbird had made the list of fifty most beautiful people in the world.

Which was just stupid. There wasn't a man alive sexier than Kit.

I shouldn't have cared. He'd ripped my heart out. God, it started with Lindsay Mack during the summer after graduation and he hadn't stopped fucking since. No, he'd started with me, then dumped me for bigger boobs, shorter skirts, looser morals. In the ten years since I'd seen him last, he'd gone through hundreds of women while I could count my sexual experiences on one hand, with a few fingers still folded down.

No man had every measured up to Kit. God, we'd been fumbling teenagers that first time in the back of his truck. It had hurt like hell, but he'd made it good, been patient and gentle even though I knew he'd wanted to just fuck. And after that, we'd gone at it like rabbits, always making sure I came first. He knew just how to set me off. It had been hot, but it had been special. He'd made me feel pretty. Wanted. Protected. Loved.

Lies. Lies. Lies.

But then it all came crashing down. I hadn't been enough for him. He'd ripped my heart out with a ruthless precision I'd come to expect from my most vicious female classmates. No one could do cruel like the rich bitches at our prep school. I'd fallen in love with him because he'd been different, but no. In the end, he'd followed in the family footsteps after all. Fuck all for money, fame and success.

I'd gone to Stanford on a full ride, heartbroken and alone. I'd studied to block the pain of his rejection, his affair. But then he'd taunted me by becoming famous. His face was everywhere. The songs he used to sing to me in the back of his truck were on the radio. I hadn't been able to avoid him no matter where I went. By then, I'd put a wall around my heart so thick nothing got through. No one with a penis was allowed into my heart. I'd turned into a cold, merciless bitch. Hell, I'd turned into one of the bitches I'd hated all through high school. I'd loved no man since, not even my husband. Which was why Robert was now my *ex*-husband.

I followed Kit's career as a friend. And despite how badly he'd hurt me, I couldn't help but be happy for his success. He'd done exactly what he'd planned. He was ruling the world with a guitar in his hands. Just like I'd always known he would.

As he looked at me, there was no guitar. There was the signature black t-shirt and worn jeans. The rakish hair, the five o'clock shadow. He was the boy I remembered. All grown up. He was *all* man now and my body responded like a plucked guitar string, coming to life with a vibrant hum I hadn't felt in years.

Damn him. I couldn't stop looking. Stop feeling...

"Crystal," Vi murmured. "What are you looking at?"

When I didn't look away, she glanced up as well. Her hand gripped my arm like a talon. "Holy shit, is that—"

I nodded.

"He's a fucking rock star. God, I have every one of Nightbird's albums. Every one of the guys in the band are hot as hell. And he's staring at you." She glanced at me. "Crystal, do you *know* him?"

Did I know Kit Buchanan? I nodded. Every inch of his skin. The taste of his kiss, the thick length of his...

She let out a little scream, but covered her mouth with her fingers.

"Girlfriend, I want the scoop."

I stared at him for one more second, then turned

away. Blinking at Vi, I tried to shake off the jolt of awareness that was wrecking me. She eyed me with an eagerness I hadn't seen before. "You really like Nightbird that much? I had you pegged for a Taylor Swift collection."

"Come on! He's gorgeous. That dark hair. And the way he plays guitar, I have to wonder what he can do with those hands. Can you imagine how dexterous those fingers are?"

Yeah, I could imagine. I could *more* than imagine.

I made a non-committal sound and she squealed.

"Not here. Not now," I whispered. I flicked one last look his way, met his heated, dark gaze. "Not ever."

I was done. Kit Buchanan ruined me once. I wouldn't let him do it again. I pasted on a smile and got on with my life, turned back to the next person waiting patiently in line. I'd seen him. I'd survived.

Picking up my pen from the floor, I returned to my life, a life that did *not* include him.

———

Crystal

. . .

"Crystal."

I knew that voice. Heard it in my dreams. Remembered it. Remembered when he'd said it playfully just before he'd kiss me. Remembered when it had been said rough and deep when he came, buried deep inside me.

I closed my eyes, took a deep breath. Turned.

Put on that fake smile I was so good at these days.

"Kit."

"Holy shit, Kit Buchanan," Vi said his name as she moved to stand right beside me, blocking him in between the table and the wall. While he could have moved her out of the way—he was well over a head taller than my pint-sized PR rep—he just gave her the usual charming turn of his lips.

"And you are?" he asked.

"Vivian Lonsdale. My friends call me Vi and you are *definitely* one of my friends."

God, she was such a flirt. Definitely someone he'd take into a back room and fuck. If he offered, I had no doubt Vi would give herself to him. She didn't mind being another notch on his bedpost.

"What are you doing here?" I asked.

He turned to look at me...and not the way he looked at Vi. This dark gaze was penetrating, as if he saw past my shiny new PR exterior to the girl he'd loved and lost. No, not lost, kicked to the damned curb.

"I saw your face on a billboard a few blocks from here."

God, I'd seen that. I had no idea my nose was so big until it was forty feet tall.

"I'm in lots of press. You didn't have to come see me in person," I countered.

"Crystal!" Vi scolded. "She's just tired. You'll have to excuse her behavior."

He shook his head, his dark hair falling over his forehead again. I itched to reach out, brush it back, to feel those silky strands again.

"No, Crystal's right. I didn't have to come see her. I wanted to." While he spoke to Vi, he kept his eyes pinned on mine. "I've been stalking her online for a while now."

My heart thumped once, really hard, as a thousand images flooded my mind. Kit, with a hundred fabulous, beautiful women on his arm over the last ten years. And none of them me.

"You guys know each other or something?" she asked. God, she was a troublemaker.

"Or something," he murmured.

His eyes turned darker and when he ran his

thumb across his chin, I couldn't miss the loud rasp. Ten years ago he barely had whiskers and now... now he was the hottest man candy ever.

"I love all your music," Vi said, clearly trying to fill the void.

"I have a concert tonight." He looked to Vi. "You should come. It starts at seven. I'll leave two VIP backstage passes at Will Call. They'll let you backstage at six so you can meet the band. Look around. I'll give you a personal tour."

Vi almost screamed. Heads turned at the way she was jumping with unrepressed glee before moving on.

"Yes, God yes. We'll be there, won't we, Crystal?"

3

rystal

I BLINKED at my friend who was going to kill me with her bare hands if I said no. Turn down backstage passes and a tour by the lead singer of Nightbird? Yeah, I'd be dead all right. I knew she was a big fan. I was one too, but only because I'd given my heart to the lead singer a decade ago, and never got it back.

"I don't know, Kit." His name fell from my lips automatically as I fought for air. Why was he here? And why was I listening to a word he said? He'd ripped my heart out and stomped on it when I was eighteen. Was I really going to subject myself to his particular brand of torture?

"Come." God, that one word from his lips made me shiver. I'd heard him say it before, but he hadn't been talking about a concert. Then, I'd been beneath him, his cock deep inside me. Or, he'd had his head between my legs, his mouth directly over my clit.

I shifted, brought my thighs together to ease the ache. God, with just one word he still made me hot. So, yes. I guess I was going to take a ride on the crazy train tonight. If nothing else, I could see what he'd made of himself. Meet the members of his band. I could finally stop wondering about his life. Maybe that would help me let him go.

"We'll be there. Absolutely." Vi's promise hung between us, thick and heavy with ten years of regret and longing and missing him.

"Look, I have to report in by four. But I'll see you both tonight." He looked at me a second longer. "It's good to see you, Crys."

Then he was gone, cutting through the crowd. It seemed he wasn't out of my life after all.

Kit

. . .

I hadn't been this nervous for a show in years. The knots in my gut had nothing to do with the thousands of fans already pouring into the arena. I hadn't been able to eat a damn thing since I saw her, since she'd called me 'Kit' in that sexy fucking voice, since she'd bitten her lip and stared up at me with those fucking baby-blue eyes that ripped through me like claws through paper.

My girl was all grown up now. And she might be hissing and snarling at me, but I saw the way her eyes darkened as she looked at me. It was still there. *It.* The completely illogical and perfect connection between us. Love at first sight, never stop wanting her, *it*. Standing in front of her, it hadn't seemed like it had been ten years since I'd had her beneath me, clawing at my back and whimpering my name. Ten minutes. Ten seconds. Hell.

I could still smell her skin, taste her sweet pussy on my tongue. If I closed my eyes, I would swear I could still feel the delicious hurt of her yanking on my hair, begging me to make her forget everything in the world but us.

"Yo, Kit. Dude, pizza's getting cold."

"Thanks, man." I nodded at Cole, who just shook his head and walked back to the dressing room to kick up his feet, eat some pizza, and watch whatever was on the TV. Our band manager, Tia, showed up with my favorite pre-concert pizza and set up enough food in the green room for a small army. A bottle of whiskey sat next to the pizza boxes on the fold-out table in the back. Unopened. Which was strange.

Normally, Reese Keeland, our drummer, opened it up and we all took a shot to help calm the nerves. Tonight, he was lying on the floor, feet up on the sofa, eyes closed like he was taking a fucking nap. The rest of the band members were draped on the furniture or grabbing a bite. Sebastian had the love of his life—a six string, pearl black, electric guitar—laying across his lap like he was going to make love to it.

I wasn't in the mood for whiskey, or anything else. It was six-thirty, and she wasn't here.

"You going to eat, or what?" Tia stepped in front of me and I realized I'd been pacing like a caged animal. I wasn't even looking forward to the show. The usual adrenaline punch to the gut was gone. Instead of fired up for the performance, I felt empty. Dead on the inside. Like a deserted back alley in a really dark part of the city.

"Not hungry."

Sebastian strummed a few chords and shook his

head at me. "What's up with you, man? You've been weird since last night."

Last night. When I saw that damn billboard with Crystal's face on it as I rode in from the airport. I'd made the driver stop as I got out and stared at the gorgeous face I saw in my dreams. *Angel.* Since the moment it hit me what a huge fucking mistake I'd made ten years ago. "Nothing. I'm fine."

Tia arched one dark, thin brow. She was five foot-nothing with a spine of solid steel. No one messed with us because no one messed with her. She could curse like a sailor. I'd seen her back down venue owners, bouncers at the seediest bars in the country, and contract lawyers. She was pure fire hidden beneath a hundred pounds of black silk hair and bad attitude. "Good. Then I'll call the front and tell them to bring back your guests."

"What?" Reese opened his eyes and looked up at me from where he rested on the floor. "Man, what the fuck? No one backstage, not this time. We're all tired, man. Who is it?"

"I'm not putting on the pretty boy act tonight. Whoever it is will just have to eat a piece of pizza and chill." Sebastian returned his attention to his guitar, and whatever new song he was working on in his head.

"Whatever. I'm not moving." Reese closed his eyes and resumed his Zen meditation pose. I didn't care. Nothing they said mattered.

"When did they get here?"

Tia checked her phone. "About ten minutes ago."

Ten minutes? She'd been here that long and I hadn't known?

"I put them on storage in the owner's office. Wasn't sure what was going on because *someone* didn't tell me."

"Sorry." Okay, yeah, that someone was me, but I didn't care. She was here. I looked down at Tia. "I need a favor. A huge, owe you for the rest of my life, favor."

She rolled her dark eyes, but was already grinning. If there was one thing in the world Tia loved, it was being needed. "What?"

I grabbed her by the elbow and pulled her with me into the hallway, and away from the band and their prying eyes. They were like a bunch of gossiping old ladies when they wanted to be. "Two women, right?"

"Yes."

"One tall, gorgeous blonde and a redhead not much bigger than you?"

Tia nodded. "Yes." I hurried toward the back

office where she'd stashed Crystal but Tia dug her heels in and brought me to a full stop. "Kit, what the hell is going on? Who are they? And why are they back here?"

"The redhead's name is Vi. She's a publicist for a major New York publishing company. The blond with her is Crystal Kerry."

Tia's eyes went wide and I knew I had her. "The writer?"

"Yes." I started walking again, eager to see Crystal. "I need you to take Vi around, give her a tour, introduce her to the band."

Her grin became more than a little suspicious. "And what will you be doing?"

"Begging forgiveness from the only woman I ever loved. Like ever."

Tia stopped moving again. "Crystal? Your Crystal? From high school?"

For fuck's sake. Were there *no* secrets around here? "How do you know about Crystal?"

Tia laughed. "You used to drink a lot, Kit. And when you get drunk, you like to talk about her. For hours."

Jesus. "Shut up. Just be my wingman, all right?"

Tia shrugged. "Sure. But you owe me one."

We opened the door and there she was, Vi's presence beside her like a shield. The office was really like a green room. An old couch, a few chairs, one of those makeup stations with a mirror and round lightbulbs all around it.

Tia rushed in and took charge like a battle hardened general and Vi was only too happy to be escorted out of the room before Crystal had a chance to blink, let alone protest that we were alone.

"Crys."

Shit, she looked good. In a pair of skinny jeans, her legs looked a mile long. Her hips had widened, a reminder that I'd hurt a girl, but before me now was a woman. She wore a pale pink top, soft and flowy, with cutouts at the shoulders. It was flirty, not too sexy. But she could have worn a sack and I'd have found her hot. Because clothes didn't matter. I knew what was underneath.

"Kit." The door latched behind me and I didn't bother to turn around. I would thank Tia later.

I took two steps closer and thanked my lucky stars that Crystal didn't back away. But then, that wasn't her style. Backing off had never been her style.

"What are you doing? What am I doing here?" The last was said with a hint of laughter. But at least she wasn't screaming, or throwing shit at me like she had before. Not that I hadn't deserved it that night. That, and more.

I closed the distance and lifted my hand to her cheek. "Fixing what I broke."

"There's no fixing this."

I ran my thumb over her bottom lip and breathed her in, lavender and cherry lip gloss. Fuck. She still wore it. The sweet scent filled my head and I knew exactly how her lips would taste, how soft they'd be. How hot that innocent looking mouth was when it closed around my cock. Her eyes fluttered shut and I knew I had her, at least for a moment.

Like a magnet, she drew me in and I lowered my head until our lips met in a tender, tentative exploration. I didn't want to scare her away. I didn't want her to run. I needed her.

Mine. Mine. Mine. She'd been mine since she was sixteen. I wrapped my arms around her and crushed her to me, all pretense of gentleness gone. How could I hold back when the most perfect thing was before me? No one compared. Ever. Her soft moan settled deep in my bones and my cock hardened instantly. I knew that sound. God, I'd missed that fucking sound.

4

*it*

She wrapped her arms around my waist as I lost myself in her taste, in the soft, wet slide of her tongue against mine. I fucked her with my mouth, exploring and tasting her, thrusting as I wanted to do with my cock. Her arms blocked me from gaining access to the rest of her body, but I rubbed her back, explored the curve of her hip. Grabbed her ass.

She had a great fucking ass. Full and round and soft, perfect for...all kinds of things.

I walked us backward until her back hit the wall and she tore her lips from mine with a gasp. Fine. I'd let her breathe, but I couldn't stop. Now that she was in my arms, it was like my entire being was starving for more. My cock pressed into her and there was no way she could miss it.

I nibbled her chin and jaw, nudged her head to the side so I could kiss and suck and lick my way down her neck. She lifted her arms to my head, buried her fingers in my hair just like she used to. "Kit."

Breathless. Hot. She said my name, but it wasn't a question, more like an *I-missed-you* sigh.

With her arms up, I had full access to the rest of her and I took advantage, sliding one hand inside the back of her pants to cup her bare ass—fuck, she was wearing a thong—and the other up under her shirt to cup her breast, to knead and tug on her nipple the way I knew she liked. Her head dropped back, banging against the wall and she arched her back, pressed into my hands.

"Kit. What are we doing?" She shuddered as I bit down on her collarbone lightly and slipped my hand inside her bra. She was so fucking soft, everywhere. Even better than I remembered.

I couldn't give her an answer, not right now. If I told her the truth, told her what I wanted, she'd tell me to go fuck myself.

I wanted her. I wanted a home, and three or four

blue-eyed babies and a couple of furry, annoying cats that would sit in her lap and hiss at me whenever I told them to get lost. The last few years on the road had been hard, and lonely. When I left her, I had nothing. My parents disowned me just as they'd warned and I'd gone to New York, found the guys, started the band. I'd lived on whiskey and peanut butter for two years, drunk more than I was sober.

The Buchanan clan was huge. I had tons of aunts and uncles and cousins, all who got along, had Thanksgiving together. I had the shit straw on that one. Yeah, I saw my cousins, almost all guys, and we'd hang, but we weren't close. When I did a concert in a town where they lived, I got them tickets. Like Natalie and Ben, along with our other cousin, Jack, who lived in Seattle. But my family, no matter how distant, never took care of the ache inside me that was uniquely hers. I was never quite assuaged by booze or drugs or women. It dulled over the years, but it had never gone away. Not until this moment.

Kissing her again, I kept her mouth too busy to ask questions. The familiar taste of her cherry lip-gloss drove me out of my mind and I realized there was no going back. Not this time.

I'd gone to California after the band hit it big,

when I had enough money to offer her something other than an apartment I shared with three other assholes and life in the back of a van. I'd thought maybe I'd made a mistake. Maybe, once she graduated from Stanford, I could fit her into my life without wrecking hers.

And that was when I'd seen the cock-sucking surfer boy and the giant diamond on her fucking finger. She'd married that asshole six weeks later and that had been it. I'd been drowning ever since. Lost, like a ship at sea with no oars and no sail. I'd written music, lots of music, and drowned myself in women to mask the thoughts of my Crystal giving herself to someone else. We'd played concerts all over the world. I didn't need my family money any more, especially with the help of my other cousin, Carter, and his investment genius.

My father had finally relented and let me come home for a visit, once I wasn't a complete failure. My brothers had my back all these years, sending me money when I was broke, keeping me off the streets. Ivy League schools hadn't made them assholes, thank fuck. My family had fallen in line, and I'd still felt empty.

Nothing got Crystal out of my head. And a year ago, I'd just stopped. No more booze. No drugs. No women. I worked. I ate. I slept. The whole band had shifted this last year. It was like we all reached critical mass and just grew the fuck up overnight.

When I saw Crystal giving that TV interview, something inside me had shifted. And when I noticed the three-carat diamond was no longer on her finger, I had become obsessed. Obsessed with what she'd made of herself. Obsessed with seeing her. Talking to her. Touching her.

Getting her back, in my life, in my arms, in my bed.

Rock hard, I squeezed her ass and lifted her off her feet, shoving her back into the wall hard enough to make the framed photos shake and rattle in place. Her soft moan drove me on and I shifted, pushed the hard ridge of my cock to the vee between her legs, rubbed up and down as I plundered her mouth.

Not one single thing had felt this good, not in ten fucking years.

Bang! Bang! Bang!

Crystal gasped and tore her mouth from mine to look over my shoulder at the door. Reese's voice came through clear as a bell. "Yo! Come on man! What are you doing in there? Jerking your meat? We're on in five. Let's go!"

Bang! Bang!

The last two blasts of sound from Reese's fist hitting the door made Crystal jerk in my arms and I knew the moment was over. I was a coward. A fucking coward. I couldn't do it, couldn't look down into those expressive blue eyes and see hate, or regret. Or pain.

Closing my eyes, I rested my forehead against hers and relocated both of my hands to the relative safety at her waist. "I have to go."

"I know."

"Don't go anywhere, kitten. Promise me." I kissed her again, once, hard and fast. "Stay. I need to talk to you."

"Is this what you call talking?" Her voice washed over me and I absorbed the moment, the feel of her in my arms, of her legs wrapped around my waist, her taste on my lips. But I knew this woman, knew her better than anyone else ever would. She was too damn smart for her own good. I'd managed to shut off that phenomenal mind of hers for a few minutes. But as soon as her body cooled, she'd be right back where she started.

Hating me.

"We'll talk, then we'll do more of this. Wait for me."

I couldn't stand there and hear her say no. Hell, I

was about to go on stage in front of eight thousand people. If she turned me down, I'd be worthless out there. So I kissed her forehead, then stepped back. Away. Knowing she might be gone when the concert was over.

"Wait for me."

Crystal

I'D HAD five minutes to pull myself together after Kit walked out. It had been just enough to catch my breath, adjust my bra, fix my lip gloss and make sure my hair didn't have the almost-fucked look to it.

God, Kit had just pushed me up against the wall and kissed me. No, he'd almost-fucked me. If his bandmate hadn't pounded on the door, there was no doubt Kit would have banged me. I'd have let him, too. The chemistry between us had always been off the charts and after ten years, it hadn't diminished.

With his uniform of low slung jeans, his tight-fitting t-shirt, dark boots, he was gorgeous. Rock star gorgeous. But that was what he wanted everyone to see. I saw the look in his dark eyes, the intensity, the need. The rasp of his voice, the way he'd called me kitten again. He hadn't wanted any woman, he'd wanted me.

I'd had my legs around his waist like a monkey climbing a tree. What the hell was wrong with me? He'd cheated on me once. He'd do it again. Kit Buchanan was a player. The king of players. Hell, he'd written the playbook for players. I was just another notch. Getting the nerdy virgin in high school then bagging her again a decade later. I should have walked away. Gone to the hotel and had that glass of wine and peace and quiet I'd longed for before Kit had reappeared. Now, I wanted the hotel and Kit. Naked.

"I'm too excited to get the details of your relationship with the fucking lead singer of *the* hottest band. For now." Tia dragged me down the hall as some tech guy with a big headset led us backstage. He told us to stand in the wing and he pointed to the stage. Not that we could have missed seeing the band. The crowd was yelling, applauding, whistling. Screaming. Reese Keeland was talking, saying something, but I wasn't paying him any attention. I was ogling Kit.

His head was down as he tuned his guitar, adjusted the strap on his shoulder.

The drummer moved into place. I knew all of them by name, not because I was a rabid fan like Tia, but because of all the online stalking I'd done about Kit. I felt like I knew them all. They were all hot in that pheromone dripping, tattoo covered bad boy way. But I only wanted Kit.

Crap. Not wanted as in now. I'd wanted him in the past. As in a decade ago.

Tia grabbed my arm and jumped up and down like a tween at her first concert.

"I see that look," she shouted as the band hit a few notes, revving up the crowd. "This isn't just a crush, is it?"

I kept my eyes on the stage when I shook my head.

"Hello, New York!" The crowd went wild.

Reese passed the microphone to Kit, offering everyone one of his trademark grins. "We're going to begin tonight with the song that started it all." He played the first few chords of *Angel* and the crowd went wild. He turned his head and looked at me, finding me as if he knew just where I was. My heart lurched, then settled. Yeah, I felt as giddy as Vi.

"Because the person who inspired the song is here tonight."

His dark gaze held mine as he began the song, sang the first line.

"Oh. My. God!" Vi squealed. "You're Angel?"

Was I? The song was about losing someone forever and Kit sang the words to me as my whole body tensed with pain. Tears gathered in my eyes and I turned my head to wipe them away. I didn't need Vi seeing this. Or Kit, for that matter. He'd broken my heart, thrown me away. And now?

What the hell was this all about? Why was I even standing her like an idiot? Was I trying to kill myself with this? With loving him again? Because he was the same old Kit. Sexy. Intense. Mine. Deep down, he would always be mine.

Kit turned his head and got into the concert. Sang and played until he was glistening in sweat, his t-shirt clinging to his corded muscles, until his tattoos were shiny and god, so fucking hot.

Had he really written *Angel* about us? I'd always thought it had been about a woman dying. That one of his band mates had lost someone in a car accident or something. But no. It made sense now.

He was telling me something. No, he was telling me everything.

I stood, rooted in place, as I watched the concert. I couldn't look away from Kit. He was good. So damn good at being a rock star. He made it look easy, effortless. Sexy as hell. And when he said goodnight to the crowd, he looked at me again. This time, it wasn't over a song that spoke of love and loss, but because of something new. Something that had never gone away. Something he had to have. Craved. Needed. *Me.*

As his feet ate up the distance between us, I became flustered, nervous. I adjusted my shirt, which didn't need it, wiped my damp palms on my jeans. All the while, he was staring at me.

"I think I'm going to come just by the way he's looking at you."

I heard Vi's words, the teasing tone, but I paid her no attention. I only had eyes for Kit as he lifted the guitar strap over his head and swung the instrument into his right hand. He shoved the guitar at Vi, not even stopping to make sure she caught it. He didn't slow when he got to me, only scooped me up and kissed me. The kiss in that office had been a warm up, a gentle introduction in comparison to this. His tongue plundered, his mouth devoured. People swirled around us. It was loud and crazy backstage but I didn't pay it any attention. I only tasted Kit, felt him, smelled him. I couldn't breathe. I didn't need to.

All at once, he put me down. His lips were slick, his eyes intent and so damn dark.

"You're coming with me, kitten."

He didn't wait for me to answer, only took my hand in his and tugged me down the emergency steps and away. Where? I didn't know, but I didn't care. I was with Kit. Nothing else mattered.

5

*it*

I HAD Crystal's hand in mine and it was like a fucking time warp. Touching her was like magic and suddenly everything mattered. Shit I hadn't cared about in forever, like whether I ate, or slept, or had any time off from our relentless tour schedule, mattered.

Time was what I needed. Time to convince her that I couldn't live without her. Time to make up for the years of hurt. I needed her, naked in my bed, and about a thousand hours to worship every inch of her body, for starters.

Dragging her out the rear security door, I

nodded at the burly guard and waved down the hired car waiting to take the band back to the hotel. We never left at the same time, and this poor bastard would be on-call until all of us were where we were supposed to be. Cole liked to flirt with the sexy groupies lined up to touch him and sign autographs for a couple hours. Reese was obsessed with his gear and would never let anyone near his fucking drums. He took them apart and put them away himself, every damn time. Tia would spend hours going over receipts and getting reports from the venue on sales figures. Riley and Sebastian would drive the sound crew crazy tweaking for tomorrow night's concert. Our last concert on this tour. Forrest and Brian would put their feet up in the green room and party with some of the girls who'd come to the show. Everyone seemed to have something to do but me.

The driver pulled up next to us and I didn't wait for him to get out and open the door. I jumped forward and held the door for Crystal like a fucking gentleman, her shy smile my reward.

I crawled in after her and pulled the door closed, sealing us in the dark cave.

"Back to the hotel, man."

His name was Chris, or Curt, or something. Something with a 'C'. But really, he was just one more anonymous face in a long line of no one. One week. One night. One hour. My life was a revolving door of people who didn't matter. Other than the band and Tia, I hadn't talked to the same person more than a couple days in a row in years. And that was pathetic. Fucking lonely. We played. We wrote music. We worked our asses off.

And then? Hours alone in a hotel room. Hours on an airplane in my own head, analyzing my life.

I'd known I needed Crystal before I saw that billboard today. Our tour was over tomorrow and we'd all agreed to take some time off. Last show. My plan had been to fly to California, find her, drop to my knees and beg her to forgive me.

But then the universe delivered her to me. My *Angel*. Right here in New York, where everything started. And ended.

"Yes, sir, Mr. Buchanan."

"Thanks."

Common courtesy was automatic, but I was already rolling up the privacy glass. The band was booked at the nicest hotel in town, and I couldn't wait to get Crystal in that king size bed, press her soft body into the mattress and make her sigh and whimper and say my name.

All. Damn. Night.

"Where are we going?" Crystal's eyes locked on mine as the flash of streetlights streaked by, alternately lighting her beautiful face and abandoning it to shadow. Her hands were folded in her lap and she looked a whole lot nervous.

"The hotel."

"Oh."

The privacy screen stopped moving with a final bump of sound and I lifted my hand to cup her cheek. I couldn't stop looking at her. Couldn't stop staring. Hell, I'd *never* stopped wanting. I ran my thumb over her full lower lip, wondered if she'd reapplied her cherry lip gloss.

"Kit, this is crazy. You know that, right?" Her voice was breathless, soft.

"No. Not crazy," I countered. "Long overdue."

That made her blink and turn away to gaze out the window. Pain. That's what pain looked like on my kitten's face. And it was my fault. I'd hurt her, badly. Yes, I'd done it for her own good, ripped my heart out in the process. But all that was over now. She was all grown up, a successful writer. I was rich, famous, and had everything I'd ever wanted. Everything but her. The weight of success over love was not equal. Hell, I'd gotten the fame but I hadn't gotten the girl.

"Why are you doing this? Why did you come to the book signing today?" She looked at me for the briefest of moments, then away.

"Can we talk about it when we get to the hotel? It's only a few blocks."

"Okay." She sighed but I didn't want her to think too much. Once that brilliant mind of hers kicked back into high gear, she'd probably push me out of the fucking car and tell me to go to hell.

So, I kissed her. Not too hard, not too crazy. Not like I was going to strip her clothes off before we got to my suite. I kissed her because she made me happy. Because just being with her made the dull ache in my chest go away. She made it *all* go away.

We were wrapped around each other when the car pulled to a halt at the curb. The driver didn't have time to give me a warning. The staff at this hotel were top notch, fast. Too fast.

The door opened and light from a string of bright lamps lining the front of the building flooded the dark interior of the car. Crystal's eyes fluttered open and she lowered her hands to her lap again, away from me. I didn't like it.

I got out, blocking the view of the bellman as I reached inside to help her onto the sidewalk. Her jeans and top with the interesting shoulder cut outs hugged every curve. Her long blond hair had come loose and curled around her shoulders in a soft, sexy wave. Just looking at her made every bone in my body ache with need.

Naked. Wet. Begging. That's what I needed from her. Soft and submissive and taking me inside that soft body.

As soon as she was out of the car, I wrapped my arm around her waist and hurried inside the hotel. We didn't speak as we passed the elaborate fresh flower arrangements, chandeliers and artwork. The elevator opened immediately and the staff greeted me by name more than once as we made our way to my suite.

Fifth floor. Balcony overlooking Central Park. Walls so thick you could play a rock concert and no one would hear a thing. The entire thing reeked of money. But Tia insisted. When we'd hit ten million albums sold a couple years ago, she rebelled and said if we were going to live on the road, we weren't staying in shit hole hotels.

I didn't care where I slept. That was the truth. As long as Crystal was with me from now on.

Pulling the key out of my wallet, I opened the door for her and she walked inside without saying a word. The draperies had been pulled back to let in the city lights and the view was spectacular.

"Wow."

"Right?" I put my keycard back in my wallet and tossed it on the small table near the door. The room was more than adequate for me, with a king-sized bed, huge television, and a bathroom big enough to park a small truck.

I wanted her, but I'd just spent two hours on stage jumping, screaming, and sweating like a damn pig. I was not going to get naked with my girl like this. And talking would lead to kissing, and kissing would lead to naked. So, yeah. Shower first. "I'm going to take a quick shower, and then we'll talk. Okay? I really need one." I plucked at my t-shirt.

She chuckled and something tight in my chest unwound, just a little. "I know."

I grinned and headed for the bathroom, pulling the door closed behind me, but not latching it. I didn't want to shut her out, and I didn't want a closed door between us. It was crazy, but I was afraid if she heard that latch click, she'd wake up from this fantasy I was in and she'd run.

Stripping in record time, I was under the water as fast as humanly possible. Every minute I was in here was another minute something could go wrong.

If I didn't smell like a sweaty, disgusting mess I would have had her naked and under me already.

The soap smelled like ginger and lemons and some other frou-frou shit I would never use, but it worked, and it was easier than packing that kind of stuff myself. I was a man on a mission, and had everything clean faster than I would have thought possible. I closed my eyes and washed my hair, sticking my head under the water to rinse. My face was in the flow of hot water when I felt her hand on my back.

6

it

MY EYES FLEW open and my cock went instantly hard as I turned to find her standing naked in the shower with me.

Fuck. Me.

"Hi."

"Hi."

She lifted her hand to my chest, rubbing in a small circle that chased every fucking thought from my head. Nothing. There was nothing inside my skull but her. But the sight of her naked body. She stepped closer, her blue eyes clouded with lust and secrets and longing. "Is it okay if we talk later?"

Green light. Go.

Hell, yeah.

My answer was to lower my lips to hers and pull her close.

Our mouths fused and I forgot to breathe. This was not the kiss of the sweet girl who'd given me her virginity all those years ago. The kiss was hot and wet, her lips demanding a response.

My cock pulsed and swelled to the point of pain between us. Her body was hot and pliant and I explored every inch of her that I could reach in some kind of frantic and pathetic need to relearn her curves, reclaim my territory. Her skin was soft, her curves lusher than I remembered.

Mine. She was mine.

I pushed her up against the tile wall and kissed my way down her body, stopping to worship her breasts, suck her nipples, rub my stubble along the curve of her hip the way I knew would make her shudder.

Dropping to my knees, I shoved her legs wide and used my hands to open her up to me, to my tongue.

Her fingers tightened into fists in my hair and her legs started shaking, but I wasn't stopping, and I wasn't being gentle.

I looked up her body to meet her blurry gaze. Yeah, she was right there with me.

There was no tenderness in me, not right now. I needed her to scream my name. I needed to feel her pussy pulse and clench down on my fingers as I sucked her clit into my mouth. I needed to *conquer*.

"*Kit.*" My name was more whimper than spoken word.

Yes. That was what I needed to hear.

I sucked and licked, sliding two fingers inside to stroke her off while I worked her with my mouth, remembering exactly how she liked it. She came all over me seconds later, her soft cries better than any song I'd ever written.

If I could make a song that sounded like the woman a man loved coming in his arms, I'd be the richest man on the planet. I could listen to that shit all night, and I was going to.

Her legs were too weak to hold her up when I reached over to turn off the water. But her hand reached for mine, stopped me before I could hit the handle. "No. I want you here. Just like this. Up against the wall, just like we used to."

Fuuuuuck.

Her words brought back the visual. Whitmore had top notch locker rooms with showers and neither one of us had ever wanted to go home. Her to a mother who drank too much, a dad who spent more time bitching about life than working. Me to Ivy League parents I could never please and the bedrooms haunted by two older brothers I could never live up to.

We'd spent a lot of time in the showers after practice, fucking up against the tile, right next to the rest of the girls' soccer team in their private shower stalls.

I used to play a game, catching every gasp and cry of her pleasure in my mouth so we wouldn't be discovered by her teammates just a few feet away.

Pointing to the tiled floor just outside the shower door, I saw the little black square. A condom. She'd come prepared. She'd wanted to be fucked in here all along. Once I was sure she could stand on her own, I opened the door enough to grab the condom, rip it open and toss the wrapper onto the floor.

"Let me," she said.

I didn't deny her when she took it from me. But when she gripped the base of my cock in her left hand and began to roll the condom down my length, I couldn't stifle the groan. Her fist was hot and snug; she knew just how to hold me. The condom was on in record time and she arched a pale brow. When her lip quirked up, I knew I had to do something about that sass.

"Turn around. Hands on the tile." My voice was deep, commanding, but she just had to say no and I'd carry her to bed and make love to her, slow and sweet. That wasn't what she wanted though, and when she did as I said and put her hands on the marble, I ran a hand down the long line of her back. "Step back. More. Good girl. Now bend down so I get a good look at that perfect ass."

As she positioned herself, she looked over her shoulder at me, watched me look at her.

Her hips were wider than I remembered, her ass the perfect heart shape. It begged to be spanked and I did just that, one playful swat. She stiffened, but bit her lip. I watched as her breasts swayed, my handprint formed a pretty pink on her pale skin.

"What was that for?"

"For being too fucking hot." I ran a finger over her pussy, pink and dripping.

"Kit!" she cried, wiggling her hips.

"What do you need, kitten?"

"You," she whimpered when I pulled my hand away.

Stepping up to her, I took hold of her hip,

aligned my dick up and slid right into her. One long, fucking perfect stroke.

"Oh god," she groaned.

"Fuck," I hissed. My eyes fell closed and my fingers tightened. "This first time's going to be rough. Then I'll learn every inch of you. All night long."

"*Yes.*"

That was the end of talking. I couldn't do it anymore. My basest needs took over and I took her hard. Fuck. Rut. Claim.

In. Out. I wasn't gentle but she didn't seem to care. The way she chanted my name and pushed her ass back against every thrust told me she wanted it. Hard.

I'd give it to her.

Damn, I wished I wasn't wearing a condom, but we had to talk first. Fuck now, talk later. Then she'd be mine and I could go bare and mark her with my cum. That had my balls tightening and I was so close.

"Come, Crys. Come all over my cock."

I wasn't sure if she came because I'd commanded it or because it was so fucking good. It didn't matter because when her tight pussy began to ripple and clench around my cock I knew she was coming. I followed her right over, my cum pumping out of me and into the condom as she milked it from me.

There would be bruises on her hip where I gripped her, but I didn't care. Neither did she. It was just another mark of ownership, of giving her exactly what she needed.

Me.

Reaching out, I turned off the water and scooped her up into my arms, carrying her out of the bathroom. That was round one. Round two would be in a bed.

7

*rystal*

"I should just let you fall into your post-sex nap and leave," I said.

I'd taken a few minutes to savor the double orgasm, but it was time to face reality. One: Kit was as good as I'd remembered. Better. Damn it. Two: He was just a one-night stand. No matter what he said—and he'd said he wanted to talk—he wouldn't change my mind about leaving. This was not a sleepover. This was not happily-ever-after. He'd broken my heart once. I wasn't going to let that happen again. So this was just sex. Really, really good fucking sex.

Kit lay beside me on his back, arm thrown over his eyes. I watched as the corner of his mouth tipped up. The rest of him? Yeah, he was naked and bare and hot as hell. His cock was still hard. And big.

"You should."

His arm dropped and he rolled onto his side. Grabbing the sheet, he pulled it up over me so my lower half was covered, although the glint in his eyes told me it was intentional when he stopped well below my breasts.

"They're bigger than I remember," he said, his dark gaze focused on them.

"Yeah, well, lots of things change in ten years."

The smile slipped.

"I've followed you in the news," he said. He met my eyes, held. "I'm so proud of you."

It warmed me to hear him say that. I hadn't gotten those words from my parents. A few friends, but not anyone whose voice held value.

"Thanks."

"Really, kitten. You did just what you said."

I glanced away, swallowed. His endearment wasn't making this easy for me. "Not all of it."

When he didn't say anything, I looked at him.

"Your dream was to get out of your house. Go to Stanford."

"Yeah, but it was also to be your wife."

If I'd stabbed Kit in the chest with a knife, the look on his face wouldn't have been as bad as this. He looked in agony.

"You married someone else." His voice was quiet.

Yeah, Robert. God, he was a mistake. "You weren't exactly an available option."

I turned to roll off the bed, toss on my clothes, but he grabbed me about the waist, spun me back. His touch was gentle, but I wasn't going anywhere.

"Say it." His eyes were darker. There was anger there, but not at me. "Say it, Crys. You've waited years to scream at me. Go ahead."

"You slept with Lindsay Mack. You made your choice."

He ran a hand over his face, sighed. "Do you remember what my parents said they'd do if I took up music?"

His parents were rich and stuck-up, more interested in appearances than people. At least they had been back then. The Buchanan name was as famous as Kit. Well, not any longer. He'd really made a name for himself without his parents' support.

"They threatened to disown you."

He smiled at that one. "One thing about them is they don't lie. They followed through, Crystal. I knew they were going to do it, too. Labor Day weekend, when everyone else had moved into a college dorm, I moved out. No money. No place to live."

God, that must have been so hard. My parents didn't care about me at all, but I'd had the shelter a full ride scholarship, four years at Stanford. A dorm room, a dining hall, all of it. He'd had none of that.

I deliberately took my time looking around the room, at this ridiculously expensive hotel room famous for hosting movie stars and Presidents. "It looks like you made something of yourself, gave your parents the middle finger."

He offered up a weak laugh. "Yeah, I did do that. I had nothing, kitten. I *was* nothing. And you? You were going places. Your dreams were all going to come true. I couldn't fuck that up."

I didn't like the way this conversation was turning. An uneasy feeling settled in my stomach. "You were part of my dreams," I countered.

He shook his head against the pillow. "No. I would have killed those dreams. Every single one. You had to go to Stanford. Show everyone how smart, how fucking perfect you are. And you have."

I jumped out of bed then, pacing the room, not caring I was naked. I looked down at the suite's fancy carpet, at the way my bare feet sunk into the soft strands. Back and forth, processing what he'd just said. I stopped. I swear my heart stopped. Slowly, I turned to face him. "You didn't sleep with Lindsay Mack."

The words were no more than a whisper, but he heard me. He didn't deny it. Didn't say I was wrong.

"Oh my god, Kit. Why?"

I started to cry then, remembering the moment he'd pushed me away. He'd ripped my heart out. He hadn't looked like a guy who'd been indifferent. He'd tried to look like an asshole, and he'd been really good at it. In my darkest hours, I'd thought I'd seen a hint of pain in his eyes, of torment, but only for a second. I'd scolded myself for imagining him in pain as he'd looked as crushed as me. But that look hadn't been my imagination. I saw it again now.

He was quiet for a minute. Ten years the truth had been hidden. Ten years he'd remained silent, let me think the worst of him when in fact he'd done it for me.

"Because you had to go. You were talking about turning Stanford down, staying with me. I couldn't let you do it."

I could barely see him through the tears.

"But—"

"Come here." His voice was soft, but I heard the steely undertones.

I moved to the bed, put my knee on it. He pulled the covers back, settled beneath them and tugged me into him. The covers went up and over me so we were face-to-face, so close I could see the dark flecks in his eyes.

"You wouldn't have left me without a good reason. I had to break your heart, and I'm sorry. But you would've stayed and I couldn't let you do that."

"It wasn't for you to decide," I countered, wiping my eyes with my fingers.

"Yes, it was. You were mine. To love. To protect, from those assholes at school, and in the end, from yourself. I couldn't let you give up your future for me."

I shook my head, the tears falling again. God, what he'd done. My heart had been destroyed but I understood. And he was right. I was eighteen and stupid. I was going to walk away from a full ride scholarship at Stanford and chase him to New York? And do what? Wait tables and try to pay for community college on my own while he played gigs?

He'd been strong, and a hell of a lot smarter than I was, at least about us. He'd loved me enough to let me go, and I could only imagine what he'd felt pushing me away.

"And now?" I asked.

"And now we have a second chance. I want you in my life."

Ten years was a long time. We were completely different people now. His life was crazy and he lived in a fishbowl, always in the public eye. Barring this promo tour, I lived a quiet, solitary life. I kept to myself, kept my head down and worked. Yes, I still loved him. A part of me always would, but we weren't just different people, we lived completely different lives. And I wasn't the kind of woman who could deal with groupies, drugs and cheating. *So* not going there.

"What about all those women?" I offered, trying not to feel jealous of all of his encounters.

"What women?" he asked and I felt my jaw drop. What women? Did he think I was a moron? A blind, deaf, idiot?

That shut the tears down. "What women?" I asked. "There are a million photos all over the internet. Do I need to Google you? I've got them burned into my eyelids, you with beautiful women practically hanging all over you. Lots of women."

"Jealous?" he asked and it just made me mad.

How was I supposed to answer that? Jealous? Yes. For years. But he wasn't mine. Kit hadn't been mine in a really long time.

My silence earned me a frown and the teasing tone faded from his voice completely. "Look, you were married. Settled down. In love. Some asshole put a ring on your finger and I was fucking jealous. How else was I supposed to deal?"

I thought of Robert. What we had was a farce of a marriage. I thought I'd be happy with him, but I'd been lying to myself. I never loved him. I never loved anyone but Kit.

"We didn't work out. I divorced him two years ago. There's... there's been no one since."

I saw the flare of heat in his eyes knowing it had been a long time, a really, really long time since I'd been with a man. Two years. Before tonight, I'd felt like I had cobwebs in my vagina.

"I won't lie, there were women in the past. But none of them mattered, Crys. I didn't love any of them. There was only you. When you got married, I had to let go. I was trying to get you out of my system."

"And now?" I asked.

He rolled us so I was on my back and he was

looming over me. His fingers stroked my hair back from my face. "Now, you're mine."

It was what I'd always wanted him to say. I'd dreamed of him showing up on my doorstep and wanting me back, telling me he was making me his. But it had never happened. Work. School. A shitty marriage and an even more painful divorce. That kind of thing washed the shiny and new off my innocence like acid on flowers. I knew what this was, right now. Right place, right time, lots of chemistry. But I wasn't a naïve little girl anymore. This was one night. Just one night. I didn't expect him to give up his lifestyle, the women, the touring, or the parties just for me. He was a rock star. He wasn't my Kit anymore. He belonged to the whole world. I couldn't compete with that. I didn't even want to try, not when I knew I'd just get my heart broken.

We'd both accomplished our dreams, but we'd grown even farther apart in the process. There was just no way I could see this working out in the long term. But I had him right now. Tonight. I could take this one night and file it away as the best night of my life. I'd think back on the sex, on his hands and his kiss and his cock, and count myself lucky for a long, long time.

When he lowered his head to kiss me, I kissed

him back like it was the last time. No, I wasn't going to sneak out while he was sleeping. Morning traffic, schedules, and the reality-suck would come crashing down on our private party soon enough. And when he nudged my legs apart with his knee and slipped two fingers into me, I knew walking away was going to be one of the hardest things I ever had to do.

8

rystal

I WOKE UP WARM. And cozy. In Kit's arms. Oh my god. Last night. Kit Kaswell.

I'd stripped off my clothes and climbed into the shower with him. I was never the aggressor when it came to sex. Never had been with Kit, until now. He'd said he'd wanted a shower and I thought of him naked, water running down all those hard muscles. I knew he had tattoos, but I'd wanted to see them. Once I put my hand on his back, he'd taken over.

All. Night. Long.

I was sore in places I'd forgotten even got sore.

My back was against his front with his cock was

pressing heavy and thick against my bottom. The arm thrown over my waist held me securely and his palm cupped my breast. A perfect fit.

"Morning," he said, his voice gruff and deep with sleep.

His hand moved, playing with my breast as his fingers gently worked my nipple. This wasn't the crazy pace of our time in the shower, but a gentle coaxing. It was working.

"Mmm," I murmured. "Again?" I asked when he shifted his hips.

"Always." Leaning forward, he nipped the spot where my neck met my shoulder. It hadn't been a hot spot for me when we were teenagers but I definitely liked it now. And he knew it. He'd known it at three in the morning when I'd woken up to his head between my legs. Wow, an orgasm was a great way to wake up.

But now, now I had to pee.

I shifted out of his hold and slid from the bed. Glancing over my shoulder, I saw him watching me, a sly grin on his face.

As I made my way to the bathroom, I shook my head at him. "You are so bad."

He pushed the covers back, gripped his cock, the

part of him that had rocked my world three times last night, and stroked it. "Damn straight."

I shut the door behind me, leaned against the cool wood. Blew out a breath when I heard the phone ring, followed by him cursing as he spoke to someone on the phone.

Real life, here we come.

I was in big trouble here. I moved to the mirror, saw myself. I looked like a well-fucked woman. My hair was a wild tangle, snarled and matted. My skin had a pink glow to it and my nipples were hard. I stepped closer to the mirror, looked down. I had a love bite on the upper swell of my breast. Kit had paid very close attention to both of them but I'd missed when he'd done that. It would be there for days.

The smile slipped from my lips. Days. I'd be gone. No, he'd be gone and yet his mark would linger. I didn't need to have the little red splotch to remember our time together. I wouldn't forget it. Ever. Just as I hadn't forgotten our time as teenagers.

It was just one night. It had been amazing, but he was going to crawl out of that bed and out of my life. I'd have to take a walk of shame back to my own hotel. Shit. I'd been the groupie he'd taken back to his hotel room after a concert and I'd be the groupie that left, walking a little bow legged, in the same clothes as the night before. And the staff at this hotel? They probably noticed everything. Every. Thing.

So embarrassing.

Kit wasn't going to give up his band and I refused to be the one to hold him back. The parties, the women, the lifestyle. God, this hotel room. I'd never been in a room like this, never even dreamt of it. The whole thing reeked of money, from the thick down duvet to the thick cream-colored carpet under my bare feet. No, this wasn't my life. It was time to go back to reality. Being a rock star was his dream, and I'd never heard anyone claim that having a conservative wife was part of the rock star equation.

And I was not the kind of woman to sit home and patiently wait while he left me for months at a time. Long distance relationships were bullshit, and I knew my heart wasn't cut out for that kind of stress. I wouldn't survive trying to do a long distance thing with Kit.

When I left the bathroom, Kit was sitting on the side of the bed.

"Tia called. A TV station set aside time for us on their noon show. I have to go."

The ache already began. The loss. This time, it

was my own fault. I'd let him in and now I'd have to live with the pain of not being able to keep him.

"I have to shower." He came up to me, stroked his knuckles down my cheek. Why did he have to be so damn sweet?

I couldn't say anything past the lump in my throat, so I just nodded.

"Give me ten minutes, then I'll get my mouth on your pussy again. One more taste before I go."

Said pussy got wet just from his voice, the mental picture of him kneeling on the floor, his hands gripping my bottom as he ruthlessly licked and sucked on my clit.

Kissing my forehead, he turned and went into the bathroom. When I heard the water turn on, I knew I had to go. Now. If he walked out with nothing but a towel around his hips, all of my willpower would evaporate in an instant.

Grabbing my clothes, I tossed them on, found my purse. I couldn't leave without telling him something. While I knew I didn't have the courage to tell him to his face—he'd just grab me and get me beneath him—a note would work. He couldn't argue with a note on his pillow.

I found a hotel notepad and pen on the desk, scribbled out a few lines.

There. Done. Closure.

With one last look at the closed bathroom door, thinking about the man who was most likely soaping up his gorgeous body hidden behind it, I walked out the door. Out of Kit's life. Out of his way.

Kit

My cock was so fucking hard. Again. I was like a fifteen year old who couldn't control it. Hell, I'd fucked her three times and I still wasn't done. I doubted I'd ever be. I gripped my cock, stroked it once, then let go. No, I wouldn't waste it in the shower. All my pleasure, all my cum would be for her. I wanted fill her up, to go in her bare, to fuck her raw. Nothing between us.

I groaned as my balls ached. Grabbing the soap, I got clean. Fast. Wrapping one towel around my waist, I grabbed another and rubbed my hair.

"Lean back on the bed and spread those gorgeous thighs nice and wide. I want pussy for breakfast," I called.

When I opened the door, I expected to see a very

compliant and very eager Crystal. The bed was empty.

"Crys?" I called, but I already knew. She was gone. Her clothes weren't strewn on the floor.

I saw the note.

LAST NIGHT WAS AMAZING. *Thank you. It was really great to see you. I have to go. Signing at two. Good luck with the tour. – Yours, C*

"SHIT," I muttered, crumpling the paper in my fist.

Leave it to a fucking writer to leave a note. I should be angry, pissed at her. I wasn't. I loved her all the more. The way I felt right now with her gone, not knowing where she was, out there somewhere hurting. I felt like I'd been eviscerated with a fucking butter knife. I could only imagine what she felt, walking away from me, from *us*. Again. This time with no lies between us. She knew I loved her. She knew I'd walked away for her, and she'd agreed that it was the right choice for both of us.

But as I stared at the empty bed, I realized I'd made a huge fucking mistake. Colossal. I only talked about the past.

I loved her now, and I hadn't told her. I'd been so busy drowning in her that I hadn't said the words. I kissed her, and I fucked her, and I forgot to tell her what I wanted.

Her. Forever. A gold ring on her finger and her in my bed every night for the rest of my life.

Fuck this. I wasn't letting her get away. My band? Yeah, they'd been my life, but they could fucking deal. Crystal was my life now. Always had been, but I'd put my music first for long enough. I had money. Fame. I could take care of her now. It was time to put her first. It was time to live. Really live. And I couldn't do that without her. I had to show her we could make this work. Following our dreams and having each other weren't mutually exclusive anymore. We weren't eighteen any longer. We weren't starving artists, or at the mercy of our miserable parents.

We could be whatever we wanted. We could do whatever we wanted. Together.

Dropping the towel, I went over to my phone and called the one person I knew could help me figure this out.

"Tia, I need your help."

9

*rystal*

VI'S HAND was like a vice around my wrist but I couldn't work up the energy to pull away. A sense of déjà vu flooded me as we walked into the crowded arena. Thousands of people were flooding the venue like a river of faces moving in a constant stream around me. Up the escalators. Down. Moving in solid streams through the corridors, everyone excited and smiling, laughing and happily standing in line to pay way too much for a t-shirt with Nightbird's album cover plastered on the front and a list of tour cities on the back. Or Kit's face.

That face. It hurt to see it on posters all around.

Everyone wanted a piece of him.

"What are we doing here? You said we were going out with some of your friends in the city." We'd made these plans two weeks ago. This was Vi's town, and she'd squealed when she saw the three-day end of the publicity tour. I was exhausted, mentally at least. And the more I tried to forget the last twenty-four hours, the more my body rebelled. I could still remember Kit inside me, kissing me, making me *feel*.

"Trust me." Vi tugged and I stumbled forward into the masses, trying to blend in. Vi had insisted we dress up tonight. No jeans. I'd been expecting a dance club with loud music, lots of alcohol and no painful memories and dressed accordingly. A tight black miniskirt hugged every curve. My heels were too high, the black straps crisscrossed over my ankle in a sexy twist that made me feel like I wasn't a total loss. My hair was down and I'd taken my time with my makeup, the armor I needed to hide my current misery from the rest of the world.

A little wine and dancing and maybe I'd forget Kit. But here? It wasn't going to happen. I might feel like shit, but at least I looked good.

I shook my head and let her pull me along behind her. I breathed a sigh of relief when we passed the security guard who admitted us into the backstage area last night. I did not need a repeat of the Kit Buchanan show. The man was burned into my soul already.

I didn't know what Vi was up to, but I didn't care much. I'd been walking around in a fog since I left Kit this morning. So, yes, I didn't see a future for us. But that didn't mean that fact didn't hurt.

A loud booming rock song started in the main arena and Vi jumped, then walked twice as fast. "Come on! We're going to miss it."

"Miss what? Vi, I know you like this band, but one concert was enough."

Would I be able to hear their songs on the radio without getting upset?

I was so not up to see Nightbird again. I should have told her about the night before, about how I'd walked away from Kit. We weren't a couple. We weren't anything. But if I explained, I'd start to cry and I'd cried enough over what *could've been* with him.

"You'll see." She grinned and I yanked backward to free my hand as Kit's band manager, Tia, came into view. She was wearing pants and blouse that made her like more like the CEO of a bank than the manager of a rock band. But, whatever.

She was tiny, but tough as nails and I respected that.

"Vi. Crystal. About damn time. You're late."

Late?

Vi shrugged. "Sorry. I tried."

Tia looked me up and down, gave an approving nod, and used a security keycard to open the door directly behind her. I looked past her to see an empty hallway lined with doors. "What's going on? Vi, I swear, if you're doing some weird publicity stunt, I'm going to kill you."

Tia lifted her hands and scooted around behind us, ushering us through the door like a dog herding sheep. I felt like I was being handled, but I didn't know what to do about it. And, in all honesty, deep down, my curiosity was at an all time high. "Go. Go. Go."

Vi stepped into the corridor and I followed her. The music was loud here, too, but oddly muffled, the bass beat thumping through the walls and ceiling, muffled enough that I couldn't make out which song the band was playing.

"Right. To the right." Tia followed us and closed the door behind her, double-checked that it was locked, and lifted her chin to nod at a giant of a security guard I hadn't noticed before. He stepped forward to stand in front of the door like we were prisoners here instead of guests.

Tia took off down the corridor, our heels a staccato burst of sound on the hard floor as Vi and I followed her.

"Vi," I complained. "Look, let's just go to a bar or something." *And forget... everything.*

She ignored me. Damn her.

It felt like we walked forever, the curved corridor stretching on in an endless loop, the end always just out of sight around the bend.

Tia walked to another closed door and used the electronic key on the security pad. When the door swung open, two large men stood on the other side. Tia greeted them and then turned, pointing in my direction. "Gentleman, this is Crystal. Can you please escort her to her place?"

One of the men held out his arm to indicate I should walk with him. What the hell was all this about?

With one last glance at Vi, whose face, for once, gave away nothing, I followed the man down the hall. Vi and Tia both fell into step behind me. With every step, the volume of the music increased to near painful levels.

Three more steps and we rounded a corner. The

man opened a small door and nodded as I walked past him... onto the stage.

Holy. Shit.

With one gentle yet solid push, I stumbled out far enough that the entire audience could see me. Glancing over my shoulder, I saw the door close behind me. I was alone. Well, as alone as I could be standing just steps from Kit with a few thousand fans screaming at the stage.

God, he looked good wearing his usual rocker uniform of worn jeans and black t-shirt.

The giant screen behind the band flickered and changed as Kit signaled the band to stop playing. The twisting psychedelic colors faded and all at once I saw myself on that screen. Me. About twenty feet tall.

Kit held up his hand and the crowd quieted, waiting expectantly. Like they were in on a great big secret and collectively holding their breath.

Kit's grin made my heart skip a beat but he didn't look at me as he addressed the crowd. "You all remember that story I told you a few minutes ago?"

Screams ripped through the arena and my hands clenched and unclenched at my sides. What story?

Voices shouted randomly from the crowd.

Marry him!

Lucky bitch!
If you don't want him, I'll take him!
Don't do it, Kit! I love you!

Before I could process, the band started playing our song softly, more like background music than a performance. Our song. The song we'd been listening to the first time we made love. The song he used to sing to me when I was lying naked in his arms. The song that still broke my heart every time I heard it on the radio. How did they know? Oh, god, Kit had told them. They knew. No, they were in on this.

Oh. My. God. What was he doing? I began to tremble. Kit loved to be on stage, showing off to thousands of fans. I didn't. I hated the spotlight.

Kit walked over and dropped to one knee at my feet. My mouth fell open.

"Crystal, I know you're scared. I know this is crazy, but I love you. I don't want to live another day without you. I can't."

The screaming escalated in the crowd, encouraging me to do everything from kiss him to kick him in the balls. Some, begged him not to do it. It was crazy. This moment was crazy.

Looking down into Kit's upturned face, my gaze found his and everything else faded. This was him and me. Us. And I saw everything in his eyes. Love. Devotion. Desperation. Need.

"The band? It might be my dream, but you're my life. Please, just say yes." He said that softly so the microphone didn't pick it up. Just for me. "We don't have to choose. We can figure this out. Give me a chance. We can have it all. Together."

The ring sparkled with an internal fire as Kit slid it onto my finger. I looked from the ring to him, realized I hadn't answered him yet. I'd thought it had to be one or the other. Our dreams or our love. He was right. We *could* have both. *I* could have both. I was a writer. I could write from anywhere. And where I wanted to be was with him.

"Crys? I love you. I've always loved you. Please, marry me." The band stopped playing and the lights faded until everything was dark but a spotlight shining on us like we were the only two people in the world.

Heat streaked down my cheeks and I realized I was crying. Everything ached inside me, the pain fierce and powerful and so damn good. I nodded, but held up my hand. "As long as I never have to be on stage again."

He grinned then, and he was beautiful. He had everything he'd wanted, just as I did. It took ten years, but it was time for us to have everything our hearts desired. We'd worked hard for it. Earned it. Deserved it.

"Deal. *Wife*."

I leaned over to kiss him, needing to share everything I was feeling with him, with the whole world watching. Suddenly, I didn't care. Let them watch. He was mine.

The crowd went crazy, but I tuned them out. All I cared about was the man who leapt to his feet and wrapped his arms around me. His lips crashed down on mine again and I was consumed by him, by this love that exploded like a bomb inside my chest, ripping me to shreds.

I had no defense against him. I never had.

EPILOGUE

*wo months later...*

Crystal

London. Amsterdam. Berlin, last week.

I sighed and curled up on the couch in Kit's dressing room on the lower floors of the big stadium. We were in London for the third concert. We'd already visited all the tourist traps. He'd bent me over the couch in our hotel room last night and blown my mind, all the while talking dirty in a British accent that drove me wild. He had a knack for adapting his voice to wherever we happened to be. I teased him that he should have been some kind of CIA language expert or spy instead of a rock star. Tomorrow, we were flying to Dublin. Irish whiskey, green everywhere and Kit promising to get me naked and talk to me with a sexy Irish accent.

That might be interesting.

The loud bass beat of the concert speakers thrummed through the floor and the walls and I tapped my foot with a smile, knowing my man was doing his thing. Sharing his passion with the world.

Laptop open, I typed. So close to finished. A few more pages and I'd be done, ready to send this baby in to my editor and take a break.

Kit was ready for a break, too. Eight weeks on tour. I'd seen some amazing places, loved every minute. But all I really wanted was Kit, a warm bed, and lazy days with nowhere to go and nothing to do. He agreed, forcing Tia to space out the dates for recording the next album. Because of me—or our newfound love—the whole band had decided to slow down. They'd been chasing their dream for so long, they'd missed the fact that they had it. It was time to live a little, too.

Especially now. Especially for me and Kit. I got the go ahead from my doc to ditch the condoms. I'd been on the pill long enough to be safe from pregnancy. I could finally give Kit what he wanted, me, with nothing between us. The next time he took me, there would be no latex between us. Nothing but skin on skin. He said he wanted to fill me with his cum, mark me. Those dirty words just made me hot and eager for him.

I was going to wait two weeks until we'd be on a beach saying our wedding vows, for our wedding night. Yeah, right. I wanted Kit in me bare just as much. I ached to know we were skin to skin. And Kit would be mine forever.

I tapped the volume on my headphones and turned them up, drowning out the concert so I could focus. This book deadline was *not* going to ruin our wedding, or the two weeks we were going to lay around on the beach fucking like bunnies on our honeymoon.

An hour later, I slipped my laptop back into its bag, done. The great thing about this job, being a writer, was I could literally do it anywhere in the world as long as I had internet. Which meant, I could travel with the band and still make a living, still do what I loved. Neither of us had to give up our dreams to be together. Vi had been thrilled for me to work and be with Kit. Hell, she just wanted permanent access to her favorite band and the hottest guys —besides Kit.

The door opened and there he was.

A rock god.

My rock god.

"Hi."

I leaned back on the couch and smiled as I spread my legs in blatant invitation. I'd just spent two hours writing one of the hottest sex scenes *ever*. Waiting for him. "Hi."

The skintight tube dress I wore was like a second skin and I was bare beneath, just as he liked. It was blue, the exact same color of my eyes, and I'd been saving the outfit for tonight, our last night in London, just to blow his mind.

He closed the door behind him and flipped the lock, the sound making me shiver with anticipation. He had no interest in the after parties, the groupies, even the rest of the band. When the concert was over, he only wanted me.

"Did you just flash me with naked pussy?"

"Yes." I raised a brow and did it again. "What are you going to do about it?"

He stalked to me, never breaking eye contact. By the time he knelt in front of me, his big hands running up and down my thighs, I could barely breathe. This moment was what I'd been waiting for all day. When the work was done and it was just us. Like this.

Up on his knees, he leaned forward and kissed me as he used his hands to push the stretchy material of my skirt up over my thighs. I was naked from the waist down, shoes on, top in place, hair and make-up perfect. The cool air hitting my wet core made me feel naughty and I loved it. Loved the way Kit couldn't keep his hands off me.

He kissed me like I was his air and I melted into him, ready to give him anything he wanted, be anything he needed me to be. Kit nibbled his way down the side of my neck and wedged his shoulders between my open thighs. "What do you want me to do about it?"

I laughed and lifted my heels to the backs of his thighs, locking my legs around him. "Rock my world."

He groaned and lowered his head, finding my nipple through the fabric of my dress. He didn't waste time. In one strong move, he pulled my hips forward to the edge of the couch and claimed my pussy with his mouth. He owned me, two fingers sliding inside to fill me up as his mouth worked my clit.

I exploded in record time, his name still on my lips as he dropped his pants and pulled out his thick, hard cock. He reached for a condom and I stopped him. "Don't need that."

"What?" His gaze lifted to mine and I saw raw lust, need, confusion. His dick was in charge of his brain right now, so I spelled it out for him.

"I talked to the nurse today. She says we're good. It's been long enough for me to be covered."

Kit tossed the small foil packet to the side and surged forward, kissing me hard as his cock slid deep in one rough thrust.

He shuddered, his reaction making me feel powerful and feminine, and like I'd just conquered the world.

"God, Crystal. I've never been bare before. With anyone. So good. So fucking good."

The slide of skin on skin was amazing and so intimate. There was nothing between us. Nothing. And there never would be. Never again.

"I love you, kitten."

"I love you, too."

And those were the last words we spoke for a long time.

———

Ready for more? Read Her Secret Billionaire next

Jack moved to Alaska for a little peace and quiet, but every week temptation arrives in the form of one beautiful but prickly Anna. Just thinking about how well she handles the stick of her float plane has him wondering how well she would handle *him*. He needs her out of that plane and in his bed.

Anna has a plan...and falling into bed with a sexy, bad boy millionaire hiding out in the woods isn't part of it. She doesn't want to fall in love with a mountain man. She wants out. She's done with the cold, the dark and the lonely nights. Her dream in the lower forty-eight is calling. Her one problem? Jack. When a storm forces her into a dangerous emergency landing, passions flare.

Being stranded in the woods with a lumberjack wannabe shouldn't be a problem. It's just one night. Right?

Right?

Click here to read Her Secret Billionaire now!

GET A FREE BOOK!

Join my mailing list to be the first to know of new releases, free books, special prices and other author giveaways.

http://freehotcontemporary.com

ALSO BY JESSA JAMES

Bad Boy Billionaires

A Virgin for the Billionaire

Her Rockstar Billionaire

Her Secret Billionaire

A Bargain with the Billionaire

Billionaire Box Set 1-4

The Virgin Pact

The Teacher and the Virgin

His Virgin Nanny

His Dirty Virgin

The Virgin Pact Boxed Set

Club V

Unravel

Undone

Uncover

Club V - The Complete Boxed Set

Cowboy Romance

How To Love A Cowboy

How To Hold A Cowboy

Treasure: The Series

Capture

Control

Bad Behavior

Bad Reputation

Bad Behavior/Bad Reputation Duet

Beg Me

Valentine Ever After

Covet/Crave

Kiss Me Again

Contemporary Heat Boxed Set 1

Handy

Dr. Hottie

Hot as Hell

Contemporary Heat Boxed Set 2

Pretend I'm Yours

Rock Star

The Baby Mission

ABOUT THE AUTHOR

Jessa James grew up on the East Coast but always suffered a severe case of wanderlust. She's lived in six states, had a variety of jobs and always comes back to her first true love – writing. Jessa works full time as a writer, eats too much dark chocolate, has an iced-coffee and Cheetos addiction, and can't get enough of sexy alpha males who know exactly what they want – and aren't afraid to say it. Dominant, alpha-male insta-luv is her favorite to read (and write).

Sign up HERE for Jessa's Newsletter:

http://jessajamesauthor.com/mailing-list/

BB

www.ingramcontent.com/pod-product-compliance
Lightning Source LLC
LaVergne TN
LVHW011848060526
838200LV00054B/4230